unraveled

C. JAI FERRY

ISBN: 1-946349-00-3
ISBN-13: 978-1-946349-00-2

Inkwell International
87779 571 Avenue
Laurel, NE 68745

www.inkwellinternational.com

unraveled

TABLE OF CONTENTS

INTRODUCTION

The stories in this collection cover a long winter's worth of written responses to various prompts, writing challenges, and contests. I was particularly drawn to flash fiction, extremely short texts that encompass an entire story in as few as 30 words. Although not every story can (or should!) be told in so few words, writing flash fiction has allowed me to unravel many of the narrative strands these characters wished to share. I hope you enjoy reading them as much as I enjoyed writing them.

Please note that a few of these stories (Story 10: Therapy Sessions and Story 19: Control) might serve as triggers for some readers. I have marked these titles with an asterisk in the text.

1

RITUAL

V anquishing frost-tipped mornings,
Seedlings seek out the gospel of the sun,
Relieving me of winter's stupor.

On day 158, I rolled out of bed as usual, took a shower as usual, and wrapped a towel around my wet hair, turban-style, as usual. I poured a glass of the same iced caffeine I'd been drinking every day, put on the same sweats and t-shirt, and sat down at the computer to start my daily routine again.

Like the previous 157 days, nothing happened. I stared at a blank screen.

I finished my caffeine, walked to the kitchen, pulled my not-so-dripping-wet hair into a ponytail, and sawed off six inches of dead ends.

And then I wrote.

2

NUMB

I chew the ice cubes, softened by my chemical caffeine, and press the splintered chunks against the roof of my mouth, my tongue molding them back into a lump that crunches once again between my molars. I remember my dentist's admonishment and cringe. But he is not facing the white wasteland on my screen. Siberia would feel more tropical. One by one, I pluck words from my veins, peppering the wintry expanse with markers to lead non-existent tourists through the hinterlands. Chewing and plucking, I create a story upon a lonely dais that increasingly feels like an icy tomb.

3

UNRAVELED

Earl rolled his rusted-out Ford to a stop in the overgrown lot. He was not a successful man. He was not a doting father, a hardworking employee, or an affable neighbor. He poured vodka in his beer cans and spent his janitor's paycheck on Pall Malls, hot dogs, and macaroni and cheese—the orange glue being the only food his youngest would eat. She'd been buying more when it happened.

Don't think about what he did to her.

Earl slid the pliers from the glovebox, gripping them until his knuckles turned white. *All because of that damned orange glue.*

4

REFUGE FROM THE STORM

The cows huddled near leafless trees, trying to protect themselves from the thick snowflakes globbing onto their hides as the gray-blue sky pressed down further. Alice ignored the cows and focused on her stove, inhaling the warm cinnamon, cardamom, and ginger steam as she poured the chai into her oversized mug. Recognizing weather—gray-blue tint for snow, green tint for tornadoes, hazy tint for help-me-I'm-melting humidity—was a deplorable necessity of country life. But she had learned. She was now as smart as a cow. She cupped her mug and smiled. Smarter, perhaps. The snowflakes weren't sticking to her.

5

MISS JENKINS

Beehive hairdos and saddle shoes recite conjugations on demand. The restless seniors do not intimidate my new arch supports, knee-length polyester skirts, and freshly printed diploma. I chaperone juniors through *Romeo and Juliet* but fail to eradicate the split infinitive from the incoming army of bell bottoms. My determination carries me forth, diagramming compound sentences across verdant walls as neon miniskirts and bouffant bangs stare back at me. Still, I am mortal. As my shoulders hunch and my skin puckers, I cannot withstand the text-message jargon invasion, until one day I am no more, erased like a superfluous comma.

6

HUNGER

Elise raced down the darkened hall, the shrieks piercing her soul. Her bare feet slid along the cold wooden floor until there was no more floor and her body bumpered back and forth between the walls, crumpling into a heap. The metal taste of blood brought the world back into focus.

Jason's night-light glowed through his cracked door. He shrieked again, the high-pitched throbbing scream rippling down her spine. Elise clawed her way up the wall and pushed forward into the bedroom. The warm yellow light from the bedside table revealed a mass huddled under Star Wars bed sheets littered with delicate-looking shards.

"Jason, baby?" Elise brushed back the covers to wrap her arms around her son, pulling him tightly to her as the shrieks subsided into sobs and tiny arms snaked around her shoulders. "It's okay, sweetie. Mama's here. Everything's okay."

"It was…eating you. They told me so." Gulps for air punctuated his words.

"No, honey. I'm okay."

He placed his tiny hand over her heart, then slid it down an inch. "From here. It's black. And ugly." He looked at her, his eyes more serious than fearful. "It's hungry, Mommy."

"Sweetie, it was just a bad dream." She pulled him into a rocking hug, as much to hide her own fear as shield him from his. He had pressed the very spot where she'd discovered the lump.

The shrieks pierced the night once more, this time echoing within her own head.

7

SHAKEN MARTINIS

The airport bar was empty when my sister finished her martini. "Dad hasn't accepted her death."

I played with my straw. "It's been a year."

"He sold the house. Welcome home." She faked a smile and signaled the bartender. "No more jet-setting for you."

I snorted. "I was teaching English in a hut–"

"Blah blah blah. At least you don't have to claim him as a blood relation." She took a swig from her second martini, watching me over the rim. "You didn't know?"

I frowned. It only took two martinis to make me a homeless twenty-four-year-old orphan.

8

TRUST

The tears were like acid on Tara's cheeks, stripping away the soot and shame as they slowly evaporated, the crusty saline tugging on her skin.

The bodies were buried under the heat of the fire, but the sweet, stinging smell of charred flesh was still caught in the back of her throat. They were her people, her community, and she had watched each one of them fighting the disease, shriveling into skeletal visions, their skin puckering as they waved her closer, leering through the spittle and blindness to beg her to use her death sticks.

And never had she breathed into their muddied thoughts that she'd been the one to bear the plague, bringing it into their homes.

Tara turned from the flames, a heatless breeze biting at her now-dry cheeks. She brushed a lock from her temple, her steps steadied, and she headed to the next unquestioning town.

9

NEW ROOTS

Your voice trickles through the phone,
cleaving our ancestral tree,
Dropping breadcrumbs from which my doubts
germinate, take root,
And spawn intoxicating fears. If not yours, who
am I?

THERAPY SESSIONS *

Lorelei reached across the restaurant's rubbery tablecloth. Just once she wished they could eat somewhere with real linens. She grasped Jeremy's hand and smiled. "I love you."

When he didn't respond, she squeezed his hand again and blinked back tears. She pictured her balding therapist swishing pompoms and cheering her on for not succumbing to the insecurity clawing its way up her throat.

Jeremy rolled his eyes. "Jeez, not with the crying again." He signaled the waiter for the check.

"I need to move on." The words popped out before she realized what she was saying. Her therapist cheered louder.

The *rah-rah-rah* in her mind was interrupted by Jeremy's derisive snort. "Like you can do better."

Her anger flared, scorching her thoughts, burning up her balding therapist mid-cheer until the red flames engulfed her, becoming white hot.

Lorelei leveled her gaze at Jeremy. "Watch me."

Jeremy followed her up the walkway to her house. She swung around to face him. "Are you kidding me?"

He held his hands out. "I paid for dinner." He stepped closer, until his face was inches from hers. "Now it's your turn to pay."

Her anger flared up again, burning its way into her brain. Her therapist was back, chanting his support. Lorelei imagined a T-rex snapping him in half.

She flashed a half-smile. "Of course." She spun around again, not waiting for Jeremy to follow her inside.

Lorelei swung the aluminum baseball bat like a golf club, feeling the bone give way with a delicate pop, like the top of a chocolate cordial when her teeth sunk into it. She closed her eyes and envisioned a golf ball sailing past a crowd of stately trees. The imaginary ball landed, bounced a few times, then came to rest at the edge of the putting green. Lorelei smiled.

She knelt down to examine the outcome of her work, resting her knee on Jeremy's chest. *Lightweight.* He'd gone down fast. Almost too fast. She wondered if her therapist had upped the dosage on her Lorazepam without telling her.

The skin along Jeremy's hairline had broken open, and blood was matting his hair. She could already see redness along his right temple where the bat had struck home.

"That'll be a nasty bruise." She felt the skin, realizing that she had shattered part of his cheekbone. "Quite the nasty bruise," she said, not hiding the pride in her voice. She patted his chest. "Not that we're going to let it develop that far."

She stood up, positioning herself once again. Jeremy moaned. Lorelei clucked her tongue against the back of her teeth. "Serious lightweight," she mumbled.

She pulled back her arms and swung once more. This time the shattering bone quickly gave way to oozy resistance. Her therapist wasn't cheering her on anymore.

Lorelei heaved a contented sigh. She was doing better already.

11

THE HUNT

Her sun-kissed face, held in hand, waits for the unspoiled,
Borne through the urban jungle by a wayward current.
Turning away, I shuffle by. Tis not I, her Romeo.

12

OPTIMISM

The dog sat, mimicking Nipper's iconic RCA pose, albeit for something much more dog-worthy than a phonograph. His tail swished through freshly yellowed leaves.

The earth behind the shed was nicely softened. The shed's faded red walls marked the edge of the withered field and the start of no man's land. The blade of the shovel struck deep.

Three more shovel thrusts and the squirrel was laid to rest between last week's opossum and the woodchuck family. The dog watched, patient as the hole disappeared.

He blinked twice, then raced out into the field. A new toy was waiting.

13

SALVATION

The reality show slipped into a commercial break, and his fiancée wiggled her hand in front of him again.

"My sister's gonna flip with jealousy." She smirked, splaying her fingers wide. "I can't wait!"

He turned back to the screen. Puppy eyes stared at him as melancholy notes seeped from the television's speakers.

She groaned. "They should just put them down."

"Excuse me?"

"It would save money." She shrugged, then readjusted her ring. "No one wants them anyway."

He clasped her hands in his, kissed her cheek, and slid the ring from her finger. He'd make a better investment.

14

LYNN'S BEST DAY

Evelyn would answer to any number of nicknames, but ski mask guy chose the one name she despised. Typical.

"Hurry it up, Lynn." He stressed the name and swirled the gun in a tiny circle, as if that would speed her up.

She gritted her teeth and shoved more cash in the bag. It was the name on her nametag. The store manager had said he was recycling, saving the planet. He wasn't. He was just a cheap bastard.

A dead cheap bastard.

Several bills slipped from her hand and fluttered around her feet. She faltered. "Do you, uh... Should I?" She pointed toward the dropped bills. Presidential faces sank into the sticky blood pooled at her feet.

"Just keep going." He circled the gun again, then glanced at the front doors.

Evelyn scoffed. "Don't worry."

He pushed the gun closer and growled, "Excuse me?"

She shoved the last of the bills from the register's till into the paper bag and froze. "I–I just meant..." Evelyn nodded toward the doors. "Nobody ever comes in this late."

Her hand was still in the bag when he snatched it from her. He squeezed her wrist through the bag and Evelyn wondered if she too would die in this shithole of a supermarket that smelled of rotting vegetables and sponge-bathed octogenarians' stale perfume. She looked up at the dark eyes staring back at her from the ski mask and held her breath.

"On the floor." Ski mask man nodded toward the floor as he took a step back.

Evelyn hesitated. They would find her body in a tacky pool of her dipshit manager's blood—all for a job stocking shelves fifteen hours a week that allowed her to escape her mother's pissed-on bedsheets.

"On the floor!"

Evelyn held up both hands and squeezed her eyes shut. "But the blood."

Ski mask laughed. It was a deep, throaty laugh that made her think of the warm salty air of an island beach. She let herself get lost in the sound of waves lapping at the white sand. If she had to die, it would be on a beach sipping fruity alcohol.

But she didn't die, and when she opened her eyes, the ski mask was gone. She stepped over the body, spitting "cheap bastard," and walked to the office, leaving tacky red footprints behind her.

The cops had to be called. Questions would be asked, reports would be filed, and tomorrow night she'd return to stock more shelves. Her mother had died more than a year ago, but Evelyn still showed up for every shift. The realization made her sick to her stomach.

She sat at the desk. Evelyn wanted out. She wanted to escape Chicago's gray winters and stupid managers who kept a slip of paper with three numbers hidden under the phone.

She slid her feet from her bloody sneakers and stepped to the safe, careful to avoid drying blood. The door swung open to reveal stacks of bills piled on two shelves. Island breezes brushed her cheeks. She was pretty sure they didn't have ski masks or stupid managers or pools of blood on the islands.

Evelyn smiled. She was going to find out.

*winner, Short Story Flash Fiction Society contest

15

FINALLY

Spring raindrops splashed across our apartment windows, splinters of glass digging into my skin.

"Where's Momma?" My voice shook.

Daddy frowned, refusing to look at me. "Be a man."

The glass dug deeper.

I saw her nearly two years later. I was eleven and had a penny for the gumball machine at Woolworth's. She was at the bus stop, chattering with some lady. She laughed as I passed by. The foreign sound startled me. I wanted to run up to her, hug her, and beg her to return, but instead I hiccupped and walked on.

Be a man!

I swallowed the hiccups and turned to study her, letting the signal box protect me. Her laughter filled the pockets of silence between the passing cars until her bus came, delivering her a final escape.

The splinters swelled into shards that pierced my chest. I stuffed my hands in my pockets and headed home, finally a man.

16

MERCY

When he said he wanted to break up, I spouted off the first thing that came to mind. "Wanna fuck one last time?" It was my one and only request for what would today be termed a mercy fuck. Not my greatest moment, but what's really sad is that it was the high point of the year-long relationship.

He said no, by the way. Politely. Unabashedly cocky—and yes, I mean that in the sense of a proud peacock. After all, his news—delivered not in the heat of the moment, not in a fit of anger, but with a gentle voice and that "I know this hurts" look—was not met with raging tears or pleas for just one more chance. I offered myself up for one last bout of raunchy, let-the-clothes-fly-and-bedsprings-squeak no-holds-barred sex and he said no.

I should feel embarrassed by his rejection, but I don't. It helps that he's gone. No, I don't mean dead—although I have spent more than a few quiet nights musing about that possibility. He's just "not here" gone. That should actually make it easier to live with my rejection, shouldn't it? Knowing that I don't have to see him at business after hours or make small talk while in line at the post office or try to hide the new pair of granny panties I'm buying when we run into each other at Target. It should, but it doesn't. My brain, in its ability to build up even the biggest loser to infinite levels of perfection, is also shamelessly brazen in its ability to invent new scenarios in which we end up running into each other. Like when he ends up in the hospital after a particularly nasty car accident and his face is so disfigured that they can't figure out who he is but they find some scrap of paper in his pocket with my name on it, so they call me down to the hospital in the hopes that I can identify him—and of course I recognize him instantly but don't say anything, instead letting him suffer in agony, alone, scared...oh, wait, this might be an example of when my brain was doing the whole musings about his death thing.

No, he's gone, and I don't expect to be running into him and sharing stories that start out "remember that time we...?" Because inevitably, I would say, "Remember that time I offered to fuck you, free and clear, no strings attached, just a good old romp, and you being the typical man naturally said...no." I know, I know, you're thinking I'd never bring up that particular memory because it's kind of shameful, right? Being rejected by a man—the creature the word "horndog" was coined for? But I would bring it up, because I'm not embarrassed. You see, I didn't make the offer for myself. The mercy fuck was for him.

17

WHEN MEMORY LANE IS TOO BLURRY FOR A STROLL

Stagnant cologne emanated from her clothes, suffocating her in the tiny kitchen. Remnants of a late-night burger were piled on the unfamiliar Formica counter. Her stomach lurched, belching up bubbles laced with last night's Stolichnaya, and she wiped crusty mascara from her eyes. Her head pulsated in a dull thud while flashing visions of popcorn ceilings and her red lace bra and her keys clanging against cold bathroom tile. She shuffled from the kitchen just as she heard a door handle click open. She froze, pleading with her synapses to connect the dots. *Just whose apartment was she in?*

18

IN THE CARDS

Madrid, New Mexico, was barely a blip on our map where we stopped to eat runny eggs and salty hash browns before stretching our legs downtown. We stepped into a mom-and-pop store with hand-painted silverware in the window. We picked through geckos carved into metal and chunks of turquoise until we found old black-and-white photographs turned into kitschy postcards for the tourists. We bought the one showing our seventeen-year-old mother wearing cheap lace. She was laughing with a man whose flattened boutonniere sagged from his lapel. Back on the road, we studied the first clue to finding our father.

19

CONTROL*

Istroked the glass with my thumb, dragging beads of sweat down the smooth surface to pool at the bottom. "Gimme another."

The bartender glanced at the full glass sitting in front of me, then leveled a bored look at me.

Fucking prick.

"The ice's melted." I threw a crumpled twenty-dollar bill on the glass-covered wooden bar.

The bartender wiped the counter down with a large off-white rag, deftly pocketing the money before he grabbed the warm drink and dumped it down the sink behind the bar. "Two parts Kahlua, one part vodka—"

"Caramel vodka," I said. "It's got to be caramel vodka."

"Right," the bartender said, nodding. "I knew I forgot something." He pulled out bottles and poured the liquids in a tall glass filled with ice.

I cleared my throat. "Two parts chocolate liqueur." Waste of my twenty dollars.

"Right, right—and a splash of root beer." He slid the drink to me across the slick counter. "Oh, and of course, your straw." He produced a paper-covered straw, holding it up to me as if it were the key to some magical city.

If only he knew.

I nodded once, which was being far more polite than I felt, snatched the straw and ripped off the paper before shoving it in the drink and swirling it around and around.

The bartender watched, waiting for me to test the concoction.

"It's fine." I waved off the inevitable question without tasting the drink, then mumbled a "thanks."

He smiled—more of a grimace, really—and moved further down the counter, wiping up nonexistent spills.

"Fucking prick," I mumbled. He looked back at me, his manicured brows raised in question. I turned away, drink in hand, swiveling on my barstool until I was leaning back against the bar.

I couldn't blame the guy for wanting to talk to me—to anyone. It was Tuesday afternoon and the bar was dead. Even the dust bunnies were bored. The lunch rush had consisted of a businesswoman dressed in a sharp pinstripe suit who ordered two olives for lunch, washed down with a neat martini. She'd kept every muscle clenched, holding her lunch in one hand and a phone in the other. It was one of those new-fangled phones that did everything—a phone, a texter, an Internet connector, a radio, an alarm clock... It likely had a vibrator as well, but I doubt the businesswoman bothered with that function. Or maybe she relied on it too much. Why bother with men when a machine can do the job?

Maybe I'm just too old-fashioned. I glanced around the empty bar. Old-fashioned, maybe, but at least not out of date. The bar was in serious need of a refresher. In its heyday, which had to have been more than four decades ago, the dark wooden tables had likely welcomed patrons to a regal, dignified establishment. *Pretentious shit.* The 1970s had brought brown-and-orange carpeting, cheap

42

gold lamps, and faded peach-and-brown rainbow curtains covering the few windows. The 1980s contributed beer posters. Near-naked women with flat stomachs and big tits hawking beer.

What was wrong with women today? They were all big tits and vibrators and absolute control. What was that term they used to describe it? Penis envy, that was it. They preferred manipulating a cold, battery-operated machine between their legs to being pliable under a man's hands all in the name of control.

Thank God my wife wasn't one of these "I can do it all myself" women. She'd been a good wife, a real woman, one who knew how to take care of a man's needs. She didn't need big tits or machines. Or control.

I winced, looking away from the posters. Big tits got in the way. I liked them little, like my wife's. Visions of our wedding flashed through my mind, her smooth, flat chest, my sun-blackened hands drag down her pearly, virgin skin, from her neck to her chest, two tiny pin pricks of nipples becoming rock hard under my calloused skin.

Stop it!

I stirred the drink and tried to control my breathing since controlling my dick was clearly out of the question. I whirled around to face the bar again, setting the drink down and hiding my excitement under the overhanging wood.

"Everything okay?"

I nodded, but didn't look up at the bartender, who started wiping down the bar yet again. He moved the rag in slow, deep circles moving back and forth along the bar, creating a slick sheen in his wake. I licked my lips as my hands itched to slide along the smooth surface, feeling the warmth of young skin as they circled down to the tiny belly button, my thumbs stroking along either side.

I shook my head, trying to clear the vision. "Another," I said, sliding the glass across the bar.

The bartender looked at me without picking up the glass. "You okay, man?"

I nodded, pointing to the drink.

"Maybe you'd better slow down. Don't want to have to call you a taxi."

Fucking prick. "I should be charging you for having to listen to such lame sarcasm."

He shrugged and poured the drink down the drain. He didn't bother using a new glass this time. I briefly thought about calling in a health code violation, then realized I'd have to find a new bar. Not worth the effort.

A new bar would bring new stresses, a new neighborhood, a new bartender to train, new people sitting on new bar stools trying to strike up new conversations. All I wanted was the old.

I stirred the drink in the dirty glass using the same straw. "It was my wife's concoction. The drink."

"Oh?" He stood watching me, holding the rag in both hands, his arms lax.

If I squinted, the rag looked like a diaper. Or maybe a loincloth. I suppressed a shudder that brought me to a full erection.

"She got me." My voice cracked with desire.

Loincloths were my weakness. They gave the wearer a false sense of modesty while making it so easy to slide my hands up underneath them, finding the wet steamy treasure below.

I shifted on my stool, trying to escape the pressure pulsating against the seam in my jeans.

"Sounds like a good woman," he said.

"She died. Car accident."

44

"Sorry, man. That's tough."

I shrugged. "Shit happens." My dick screamed in protest at my nonchalance. I hadn't had a steamy treasure since she died. I was overdue.

"How long's it been?" he asked.

"We're doing the one-year memorial service tonight at the kids' house." She had been the only one to understand me, to help fill my needs, even the darkest ones. And she had never batted an eye at my requests, never lorded it over me, never tried to control me.

"Being with family is good," he said. "Gets you through the tough times."

I dropped the straw in the drink, reached into my back pocket, and pulled out my wallet, flipping open to the family picture.

"Good looking bunch," he said.

"Yeah." I stroked the picture with my thumb. It had been summer when we took the picture, and the granddaughter had been wearing a bright yellow tank top and cotton shorts. I rubbed my thumb up and down, still feeling the tight seam of her shorts running between her legs. She had been the last treasure my wife had brought me, her breath still smelling of the Kahlua-chocolate-alcohol mixture.

"Won't be the same without her," I said shoving the wallet back in my pocket. The throbbing from the front of my pants screamed at the unfairness of it all. It didn't want to share its limited space. It wanted to go back to the way it was, to be free to indulge. *To be a fucking prick.*

I reached down and gave it a light patting, commiserating our unfair sentence.

20

ADMISSIONS

I fingered the hospital gown's hem. "He's dead?" I studied the officer.

The cop shifted, glancing at the doctor.

My hand trembled. "Why don't I remember?"

The doctor rested a hand on my shoulder. "We've called a specialist."

I rubbed my temple. "There's just…nothing there." I scowled.

The doctor escorted the officer from the room.

I chewed my bottom lip. *Nothing I'm ever going to admit to.*

21

_____

BAGGAGE CLAIM

She chewed the last ice cube, letting the crunching fill the bubble of silence segregating her from the homecomings. God, she hated airport arrivals. They were like expensive candies: decadent, savory, gluttonous. She swallowed the shards of ice, pushing them past her rising indigestion as a smooth voice announced the last arrival from the coast. She scanned the faces. His was not among them. She tossed her empty cup in the trashcan and headed for the exit. Neiman Marcus was still open. She'd fill up his space with some new Oscar de la Rentas, Jimmy Choos, and indulgent candies.

22

LAW AND ORDER AND DOMINION

J ack wanted to pull against the cuffs. *Rule #1: Do not resist.* He focused on the linoleum floor at his feet, a vomitus green remnant from the eighties. *Rule #2: Do not make eye contact.*

"What the—?" The judge glared at the prosecutor. "Littering?"

The twenty-something prosecutor stood his ground. "We're asking the max. Three months, $500."

"For cigarette butts?!" The judge snorted, then growled at Jack. "You—quit smoking."

Jack nodded. *Rule #3: Show remorse.*

"You—find some real goddamned criminals." The gavel crashed down. "Dismissed!"

Jack shuffled by the judge. *Rule #4: Be grateful.* "Thanks, Pop."

23

THE CHOICE

Samara knew she was sleeping, which meant she was dreaming, but nothing about it felt like a dream. She walked through a field, her bare feet sinking into the wet ground. Cool mud oozed between her toes. There was no sun in the sky, but there was a hazy grey non-light, as if she was halfway between day and night. She could still see everything around her and smell the rain on the air. She reached out to run her hands through the waist-high grasses, but jerked back when the edge of a blade caught on her finger. She brought her hand to her mouth. The coppery taste of blood mixed with her saliva. Still, she moved forward.

She could see them in the distance. Twelve wooden doors, each painted a different color. Some were pastels, like brightly dyed Easter eggs. Others had a metallic sheen. One was so black it was almost impossible to see. She moved closer, hoping they were some sort of art installation, convinced they were there for her.

Samara slowed when she saw an old woman sitting in a rocker. The woman's milky eyes stared blankly toward the horizon while her gnarled hands worked rusted knitting needles, her wrists flexing back and forth. She paused her knitting and cocked her head, turning her face to the right. "You must choose." She ran a hand along the air, as if smoothing out her knitting, but there was no yarn in the needles.

Samara frowned. "Why?"

The old woman swung her head around to the left as she made a hacking sound, and Samara realized she was laughing. "You're a precocious one."

The old woman coughed to clear her throat, her drooping shoulders jerking forward so violently that Samara held up her hands as if to stop the woman from falling out of the rocker.

The coughing fit passed, and the woman resumed her invisible knitting, again staring at the horizon. "Choose."

Samara crossed her arms. Her frown deepened. "Not until you tell me why."

The woman whipped her head up to stare at Samara, and her milky white eyes darkened to a deep onyx. "Do not take such an attitude with me, child." Her voice boomed all around Samara, who blinked against the woman's stale breath rushing past her cheeks. The hazy sunless sky flickered through several shades of darker grey. The hair on Samara's arms stood up as if electrified. "Now, choose!"

The girl did not back down, although she did tighten her arms across her chest and dig her toes deeper into the mud. "What if I'm wrong."

One eyebrow arched. "What if you're right?"

The old woman stood and disintegrated into thousands of Blue Morpho butterflies that rushed at Samara, who lifted her arms to ward them off. She squeezed her eyes closed, trying to ignore the wings beating furiously against her face and arms and getting tangled in her hair.

"Enough!" she screamed.

The beating stopped, and everything became still.

Samara opened one eye slowly, then opened the other and lifted her head. She was back in her bedroom, standing at the foot of her bed and facing the window that looked out over the field. The full moon lit up the world before her, and in the distance she saw twelve trees swaying in a gentle breeze.

She sat on the edge of the bed. "That's it. No more late-night tiramisu." She took several deep breaths to calm her racing heart, but when she looked down at her feet, her heartrate spiked again. They were covered in mud.

24

WINTER

I race from the medical receptionist's cloying perfume to gulp in the icy parking lot air. I study the precise landscaping, my ears burning. The now-dead branches will soon birth new life, but my belly will only breed jealousy.

25

SAVED BY PINK CHIFFON

Nobody called on my birthday. They didn't send me birthday cards or well wishes in an email or even a shout-out on Facebook. I spent most of the day alone, wallowing in my own self-pity and wondering what kind of horrible person I must be to not warrant a single celebratory wish. I was clearly a friendless, childless abomination who did not deserve a celebration. That night, I cried into my pillow that I was doomed to live a meaningless life only to be forgotten as soon as the ink dried on my death certificate.

The next day, I told myself that if my friends were going to bail on me, I would find meaning in myself and a piece of the local café's decadent cheesecake. I put on a simple cotton dress and walked to the café to give myself time to decide whether to indulge in the sweet raspberry drizzle to go with my birthday cake. I was just a few doors away from finding the rich meaning I craved when I saw a golden flash race across the sidewalk ahead. Tires squealed, ending in a thick thud. For a moment, the world around me slowed, and my own breathing was heavy in my ears. Burned rubber flooded my nostrils, mingling with the yeasty aroma of fresh baked bread from the café. Then the screams erupted, bringing me back to normal speed.

Like everyone else, I rushed forward.

"Call 911."

"What was he doing in the street?"

"Is he breathing?"

"Don't move him."

We stood, helplessly gawking at the scene. A woman—too young to be the boy's mother—wailed over the body. The driver of the van stood several feet away, shifting on his feet. Fear tugged on his cheeks, and his eyes swelled at the reality before him. He licked spittle from the corner of his mouth, and I knew his fear was genuine, although it was a fear housed in self-preservation. He stared at the front of the van, which was splattered with blood. The same blood was drizzled in the golden hair of the child under its bumper.

The woman next to me, a heavy-set mouth-breather who smelled of cheap perfume and self-loathing, elbowed me out of the way as she jockeyed for a better position. She had her iPhone out, recording it all. Behind me, two college kids pointed out the details of the accident: the dent in the van's bumper, the odd angle of the boy's body, the missing shoe.

I strained to peer over the shoulder of the wailing woman and saw a white sock, its bottom as dark as the pavement. Why had this little boy, in his final moments, been wearing such dirty socks? The question latched onto my brain, and I couldn't shake free of it. I began shifting with the crowd of onlookers, pulsating forward to get a better understanding of the tragedy so we could share it on our blogs and Twitter feeds and Facebook. We had to know, had to share, had to inform the world of the self-awareness gleaned from being in the right place at the wrong moment and bearing witness to a child's final breaths.

And, yes, he was still breathing. Despite the unnatural bend in his back and the raspberry splatter behind his head, this boy, this child, he breathed! But it was like no breath I had ever heard before, garbled as it was with a throaty gurgle of spit and blood and hope-drowned-in-realization. I pressed forward, moving past the iPhone-wielding woman and her snide "excuse you" to kneel next to the wailing woman who could not be the boy's mother. I rested my hand on the boy's sock-covered foot, and he slid one tear-crusted eye over to look at me.

He shuddered and let go.

I almost begged him to take me with him.

The paramedics arrived, but they had no urgency in their step. They moved the wailing woman to the back of their ambulance. A police officer spoke to the driver, whose hand-wringing and cracking voice shouted out his fear for all to hear. He would lose his job, lose his home, lose his family. I bit my tongue before pointing out that his socks would still remain a crisp pristine white. The boy's body was covered and removed, the van driver was escorted away by the police officer, the wailing woman's cries were reduced to whimpers, the van was moved to allow traffic to flow once again, and the gawkers went back to their afternoon shopping.

I blinked, and the traumatic scene was gone, leaving me to question if I'd really witnessed it at all. But even from the sidewalk I could see the blood-stained asphalt. Cars moved over it, and I wondered if the people driving by knew they were taking pieces of the little boy home with them. The thought of raspberry-drizzled cheesecake turned my stomach, so I walked back the way I had come.

The dog was sitting on my stoop when I got home, as if keeping watch, although for what I had no idea. When he saw me, he cocked his head to the side. He was an all-white version of Nippy the RCA dog, and apparently I had become the phonograph. I watched him watching me as voices in my head warned me to run, move slowly, avoid eye contact, and back away. I gave them an internal eye roll and sat beside the dog, draping an arm across his back. The dog shifted, turning his back to me while scooting closer into my hip. A flash of crimson startled me, and I jumped up, worried that I was about to witness yet another soul passing, but the dog looked up at me, his mouth spread open in a surreal laugh as his giant tongue lolled to the side.

He stood up to face me. The color was not the tell-tale red, but a deep pink chiffon tutu wrapped around the dog's backside. He turned in a tight circle, showing off his outfit, then sat once again, looking up to me. A small blue heart hung from his collar. His name was Brewster, and Brewster had a phone number. The line was busy.

Brewster went inside for a bowl of water and a nap on the couch while I flipped through the channels on the television. It didn't take long for the picture of the blond-haired boy to appear, along with details of the accident. His name was Nathan. He was six years old. He loved watching the movie *Cars* and playing on the swings with his older sister. I muted the sound and stared at the photos that crossed my screen. One shot in particular caused the breath to catch in my throat. A younger Nathan sat in front of a Christmas tree, his eyes wide as he stared up at Brewster.

I called the number again. Still busy. I found the family's address online. They lived only a few blocks from me. I woke Brewster up and called him to the door, but he stayed on the couch, turning his head first one way, then then other. Finally he dropped his head to rest on his crossed front paws. I tried to push Brewster off the couch, but the dog was stubborn. I offered him cubes of cheese and leftover Kung Pao chicken. I swear he laughed at me.

The third time I tried the number, a man answered, his voice scratchy and raw. I told him I'd found Brewster. He said Brewster liked bone-shaped treats, but he was an escape artist. His voice cracked, and he wished me luck before hanging up.

I stared at the dog on my couch, the pit bull in the pink chiffon tutu who refused to budge. I imagined his doggie friends laughing at his ensemble, their snickers and hushed whispers and mocking looks driving him to run away. I sat next to Brewster, who dropped his heavy jaw onto my lap in an almost protective pose. Why had he run away when he had Nathan, a loving friend, to chase after him? But now Nathan was gone, and Brewster was forgotten, tossed out without a parting glance.

I couldn't blame Nathan's family. My own little Nathan had been flushed down the toilet just weeks after my body created him, without me understanding what was happening. I'd been heartbroken, although I couldn't explain why. It was just a glob in my gut, not a living, breathing, blond-headed boy running around in dirty socks. I broke up with my boyfriend, unable to push away the thoughts that he was responsible for me feeling such pain. Rubbing Brewster's head, I knew Nathan's family would come to hate the pup, just as I hated my boyfriend for shrugging it off and leaving so easily.

I would not abandon Brewster in his time of need. I would not be one of those people, not again. I slid off the couch and went to the bedroom closet, where I dug around in the boxes in the back until I found my Halloween costume from three years ago. As I freed the box, I promised myself I would scratch Brewster's belly and take him for rides in the car with the windows rolled down. Inside I found the pink tutu I'd worn as part of my drunk ballerina costume. I slid it on over my dress and turned around to see Brewster sitting in the doorway, watching me and studying the addition to my outfit.

And then he wagged his tail.

26

A LOVE STORY

I held up his ice cream. The pup sniffed it before sticking out his tongue for a lick. His tail wagged. He eyed me while his tongue darted out again.

When his head started shaking, I pulled the cup away, almost expecting his teeth to be chattering. He sat, adopting his polite "I'm waiting for you" pose. He didn't seem to mind the brain freeze.

I held the cup out again. This time, he skipped the licking, instead gulping down the soft-serve in three bites.

He licked the cup clean, then noticed my dessert. His eyes were my Kryptonite.

ACKNOWLEDGMENTS

They say that writing is a solitary endeavor, but I have not found this to be true. Through writing, I have been introduced to various communities of readers and writers who cheer me on, prod me in the darkest hours, offer insightful feedback, and provide forums full of engaging discourse.

One person who has continued keep the welcome mat out, despite what she might be facing in her own life, is Charli Mills, who has built an amazing community of flash fiction writers at the Carrot Ranch. If you enjoy reading flash fiction, then you definitely want to check out the Congress of Rough Writers on her website (and make sure to sign up for her newsletter and you will get a weekly dose of 99-word stories centered around a specific theme delivered to your inbox).

I also want to thank Diana Nagai, who unexpectedly offered extremely kind words that spurred me to get this book off my to-do list and on to my completed list.

Finally, to all the beta readers and people who support my writing addiction, thank you!

ALSO BY C. JAI FERRY

THE HONEYSUCKLE COLLECTION
Honeysuckle Road • *Honeysuckle Memories* • *Honeysuckle Dreams*

When I was in first grade, my family lived in an enormous city in the south. My memories of that city are crowded with cars honking and people talking incessantly. I just remember noise. But a few blocks from my house, the river channel was surrounded by honeysuckle bushes, and we would pick the flowers from the bushes and suck on the sweet nectar. It was a haven of calm while the world raged on "out there." Those honeysuckle bushes are long gone, but the feelings they evoked remain with me and often peek through in my writing. The stories in the Honeysuckle series focus on people dealing with some intense emotions as they face changes at the core of who they are. Some rage against the changes being forced on them, others embrace the changes, but somewhere along the way, they have a fleeting moment of detachment, a brief interlude when they too are able to enjoy the honeysuckle nectar.

"Skeleton Dance"

Skeleton Dance, the winner of the 2014 Vermillion Literary Project Short Story Contest, tells the story of a young girl who must survive the eccentricities of her grandmother after the death of her mother. Also look for the short film *Skeleton Dance*, directed by Benito Garcia.

The Life of Me

A collection of short stories and poetry that explores how one's perceptions are influenced by their surroundings.

ABOUT THE AUTHOR

C. Jai Ferry grew up in a small rural town in one of those middle states between New York and Los Angeles. She focuses on short stories with narrators who are often described as brutally honest and who likely need some form of professional help. If you've enjoyed these stories, please leave a review. Thank you!

Check out all of C. Jai Ferry's novels, short stories, and ebooks as well as free stories and what's coming next by visiting www.cjaiferry.com.